DONKEY-RIDE TO DISASTER

Part One in a crazy four-part adventure ...
Poor old Nev Niceguy. His job as a
humble woodcutter barely puts food on
the table—and now he and his dotty
old Gran owe YEARS of back rent! If
they can't find the money, they're out
in the forest ... What's a Niceguy to
do? Armed with 43 sandwiches and his
trusty axe, Nev prepares to go it alone;
to seek out and bring home one
hundred gold coins. But will he survive
the big wide world?

DONKEY-RIDE TO DISASTER

Kaye Umansky

Galaxy

CHIVERS PRESS
BATH

First published 1999
by
Hodder Children's Books
This Large Print edition published by
Chivers Press
by arrangement with
Hodder Children's Books
2001

ISBN 0 7540 6184 1

British Library Cataloguing in Publication Data

Umansky, Kaye
    Donkey-ride to disaster.—Large print ed.
    1. Debt—Juvenile Fiction 2. Prisoners—Juvenile
Fiction 3. Humorous stories 4 Children's stories
    5. Large type books
    I. Title II Fisher, Chris
    823. 9'14[J]

ISBN 0-7540-6184-1

Printed and bound in Great Britain by
BOOKCRAFT, Midsomer Norton, Somerset

CONTENTS

For Mo and Ella

CHAPTER ONE

THE WOOD

Neville Niceguy was having a fantasy. He was a woodcutter, deep in a dark forest, hard at work chopping down a small tree. All at once, there was a flash of light, and a lovely fairy in a blue net frock appeared, handing him a big bag of money!

'Here, Neville,' she said. 'This is all yours. You will never have to chop another tree again. And by the way, us fairies think you're *very* handsome.'

Eagerly, he reached for the bag—he nearly had it—almost—and then—

'Well, well,' said a sneering voice. 'If it ain't young Neville Niceguy.'

The fantasy shattered. The fairy flashed him a sad little smile and vanished, taking the money with her and—to Neville's bitter disappointment—he found himself standing ankle-deep in wood chippings with an axe in his hand. What a drag. He really *was* a woodcutter. The fairy had been the fantasy part. The reality was that he had company: Malc, Ginge and Kenny, no less.

Malc, Ginge and Kenny were woodcutters too. Usually they worked over on the west side of the forest—but every so often they took it into their heads to wander over and annoy Neville. Malc was big and muscular, with two crossed axes tattooed on his upper arm. Kenny was small and weasly. Ginge was—well, ginger.

2

'What was you smilin' at, Neville?' enquired Malc. 'Mm? Standin' there grinnin' into space like a great daft Nelly.' Ginge and Kenny snorted down their noses.

'Nothing,' said Neville.

'Seein' things, are we?' said Malc. 'First sign o' madness, that.'

'No it ain't, Malc,' put in Kenny, then immediately wished he hadn't.

'You what?' said Malc, with a frown.

'Seein' things ain't the first sign o' madness, Malc. That's talkin' to yerself. Or so I 'eard.'

'Shut up,' said Malc. 'Don't contradict me. I'm talkin' to Neville.' He leered into Neville's face. 'Neville,' he repeated. 'It's a silly name, ain't it? Neville. Neville, Neville. Ne—ville.'

'Sounds a bit like devil,' said Ginge. 'But with a nuh. Instead of a duh.'

'Oh, but Neville ain't *devilish*,' continued Malc. 'Dear me, no. He's more of what you'd call a goody-goody. Nice little niddy noddy nerdy Neville. Wot suffers from nerves. *Nerville.*'

'Ha, ha, ha!' crowed Kenny, trying to get back in favour. 'Nerville. Brilliant. I get it.'

'Ha! ha! Yeah,' agreed Ginge, who didn't.

Malc's mean little eyes lighted on Neville's lunch, which was neatly wrapped in a spotted hanky and lying on the ground next to his jerkin. 'Oooh, look! It's his sandwiches, what his dear old granny made. What's it today, I wonder? Somethin' posh, I'll bet. *Coo*cumber, d'you fink? In little

4

*tri*angles? Wiv the *crusts* cut orf?'

' 'Spect you'd like one o' them posh sandwiches, eh Malc?' chipped in Ginge, keen to be part of the humour of the situation.

'I might indeed,' agreed Malc. 'Ho yes. We 'eard you choppin' from afar, Nerville. 'Ark, I said. That's Nerville Niceguy. Let's stroll over, I said, an' 'ave a friendly little chat. See 'ow 'e's gettin' on. Right, boys?'

'Right, Malc,' sniggered Ginge and Kenny. 'That's what you said.'

'So let's 'ave a looksy.' Malc strolled over to Neville's cart and examined it with a professional air. Venetia the donkey looked up and gave him a dirty look.

'My, my,' said Malc. 'Oo's been a busy boy, then? You got 'arf the forest 'ere. Only the *tiddly* little trees, I notice. But then, you'm only a tiddly little chap.' He took out a pocketknife and began to clean his finger nails. 'Looks like you'm 'avin' trouble with that little feller, mind.' He nodded at the tree that Neville was working on.

'It's a tough one, yes,' agreed Neville. It was, too. That's why he had stopped for a moment and allowed himself the quick fairy fantasy. He was exhausted.

'Stand aside,' ordered Malc. 'I'll show you 'ow it's done. It so 'appens I'm in a good mood today.'

He made a great show of unshouldering his axe. Then, with a broad wink at the others, he elbowed Neville aside and swaggered up to the tree. He spat on his hands, grasped the trunk and snapped it off just as easily as picking a daisy.

'There,' he said, tossing it into the cart with a grin. 'See 'ow good I am to you? Now.' The grin vanished and his brow darkened. ' 'Ow about them sandwiches?'

Neville knew when he was beaten. 'Help yourself,' he said, with a shrug.

Malc scooped up the bundle and untied it.

'Oh *dear*,' he said sadly, shaking his head. 'Only bread and drippin'. Not up to my usual standards. There's none o' them little halves of tomato with the wiggly edges. No nice little treats. I must complain to the chef.'

'You should be a stand-up comic, Malc, you really should!' gasped Ginge, clutching his sides. Playing for laughs now, Malc continued to rummage through Neville's lunch.

'Ooh, I tell a lie! Look what I found! *It's a lickle gingerbread boy with no 'ead!*' Triumphantly, he held it up.

'Yes, it 'as, Malc,' interrupted Ginge.

' 'As what?'

'It 'as got an 'ead, Malc, wiv little currant eyes and everyfin'. Look.'

Malc raised the gingerbread boy to his mouth and took a large bite.

'I don't see no 'ead,' he said, chewing. Ginge and Kenny laughed so

7

hard they nearly died. Neville bit his lip and said nothing.

'So,' said Malc, spraying crumbs everywhere. 'I 'spect that'll be you done fer the day. You'll be off to the sawmill, I 'spect. If that wonky old cart of yours'll make it.' He swallowed the last of Neville's lunch, burped loudly and blew his nose on the cloth. ' 'Ere. Catch!' He screwed it up and chucked it at Neville, who missed. The cloth fluttered down into the mud.

To muffled titters, Neville collected his jerkin, threw his axe into the cart, climbed up and picked up the reins. Venetia twitched her ears and set off up the familiar trail without even bothering to open her eyes.

' 'Bye bye, *Ner*ville!' shouted Malc. 'Tell yer gran I'll 'ave chicken tomorrow! I'm partial to chicken!'

Trying hard to ignore the jeers ringing in his ears, Neville rounded the first bend. He fumbled at his feet for the long, bendy stick with the carrot dangling on the end of the string.

'Come on, girl,' he muttered to Venetia. 'Let's go while the going's good.'

Five minutes up the steep slope he began to relax. All right, so his lunch had been pinched again—but things could have been worse. At least Malc had been in a good mood. Sometimes his friendly little chats got much nastier than that. Sometimes they ended with a friendly black eye, or a friendly arm twisted up the back. Yes, on the whole, he'd got off lightly. After all, the sun was shining and he had a full load.

Another hour, and he'd be back home with a shilling in his pocket, eating his tea.

'*Blue skies shining at me,*' sang Neville. '*Nothing but blue skies do I . . .* aaaaaagh!'

CHAPTER TWO

THE COTTAGE

'They did *what*?' gasped Gran.

'Cut the traces,' said Neville gloomily. 'Malc must have cut them part through with his knife when he was over by the cart. Or maybe it was

13

one of the others. All I know is, I was halfway up the slope, and suddenly Venetia was going forwards and I was going back! I tried to jam on the brake, but it came off in my hand. Then a wheel went in a ditch and the next thing I knew I was lying in a bush being looked at in a funny way by this squirrel. I reckon I got off lightly with a bruised thumb.'

'Tsk, tsk, tsk,' tutted Gran. 'That was very naughty of Malcolm. He's always been trouble, that one. I'll have a word with his mum, so I will. I expect she'll give him a smack.'

'Er . . . I don't think she will, Gran,' said Neville. 'But thanks anyway.'

'Well, I'm not having you bullied like that.'

'I can handle it, all right? Anyway, it's a whole day's wood wasted, and no shilling. And the cart's had it. We'll have to get a new one now.'

'Mmm,' said Gran, vaguely. 'How about another scone? I made them specially, with the last of the flour. I think there might be a scraping of honey left . . .'

She hobbled to the dresser and peered at the neatly labelled jars. Most were empty. Neville came up behind and tapped her gently on the shoulder.

'Did you hear what I said? I'll have to go over to Carter's tomorrow. I'd get a bigger one if Venetia could manage it. What do you think?'

'Oh, you can't do that, dear,' said Gran. 'There's no money, you see.'

Neville suddenly got a *bad* feeling.

'What d'you, mean, no money?' he enquired, slowly. It wasn't possible. There must be *some* money. 'What about our savings? In the old teapot?'

'All gone. I gave it to this poor old tramp. You should have seen his coat, Neville. It was a disgrace. No buttons, hem hanging down, patched all over . . .'

'How much?' asked Neville. 'How much did you give him?'

'Whatever was there, dear!' cried Gran. 'I don't know. Ten guineas or something.'

Ten guineas?

'Don't you think,' said Neville, choosing his words carefully, 'don't you think that, perhaps, ten guineas is rather a lot to give for an overcoat?'

'Well, I thought he could get a nice shirt as well. Charity begins at home, don't forget. Food on the table and a roof over our heads, that's all that matters. Which reminds me.'

She reached behind the clock and handed him a bundle of letters. They were addressed to: *The Occupier, Plumtree Cottage, Fingle Forest.*

'What are these?' asked Neville. The bad feeling was getting stronger.

'Reminders from Old Squire Skinnard. Him with the funny leg and

the smelly old pipe, remember? When you was little, you used to run and hide when he came rent collecting. 'Course, he's too doddery to come and get it himself now, so he writes letters instead. He's been sending them quite regular. I think we might owe him a bit of back rent. Now, you sit yourself down and I'll see if there's a bit of cake left . . .'

With a sinking heart, Neville began to leaf through the envelopes. There were dozens of them.

'You haven't opened any of these,' he said.

'That's because they all say the same thing. I opened some of the earlier ones, but they were so rude I chucked 'em in the bin. Ah! Here we are! A slice of plum pie. It's past its best, but if I scrape off the green bits . . .'

Neville let her ramble on. With rising alarm, he peered at the dates on the envelopes. They went back months. No, years! *They went back years!* The older ones were beginning to turn yellow. One of them had been used for a shopping list. It had *crumpets* written on it. He couldn't remember the last time they had eaten crumpets. The two oldest envelopes at the bottom even had a dead spider squashed between them. He selected the one that bore the most recent date, ripped it open and silently studied the contents.

Oh dear.

'Gran,' he said slowly. 'You're right. These are from the Squire.'

'Oh, yes?' said Gran. 'And what does he say?'

'He says that unless the arrears are paid up within one month, he'll repossess the cottage. We're about to be evicted!'

'Mm,' said Gran, vaguely. 'Now then, shall I top up the teapot, or make some fresh? Or course, we haven't got much

18

tea left now . . .'

'How much?' asked Neville.

'About half a cupful . . .'

'No. How much are the arrears? How much do we owe?'

'I'm not really sure, dear. I'd have to check the rent book. I do hope this pie's all right . . .'

'*How much*, Gran?'

She gave in.

'One hundred gold coins.'

'*Whaaaaaaat?*' His horrified cry rang around the rafters of the tiny kitchen.

'There, you see?' said Gran. 'Now you're cross with me.'

She was standing by the dresser with a small, sad slice of pie on a plate. She had done her best to make it look appetising. It was curling up at the

edges, but she'd gone to the trouble of putting it on a doily. Poor old thing. She couldn't help being a bit vague these days, forgetting to pay bills or pick up change and always losing her purse and giving away their life savings to tramps.

'I'm not cross.'

'Yes, you are. I'm sorry, dear. I didn't realise you needed a new cart.'

'I'm not. Really. It's just that I had no idea we were this much in debt. I wish you'd told me, that's all.'

He read the letter again. One month. How would they ever raise all that money *in one month*? The cupboard was virtually bare, the cart was a heap of matchwood in a ditch and he didn't think he could chop wood anyway with his bad thumb.

'I've done wrong, haven't I?' said Gran, pathetically dabbing at her eyes with her apron.

'Hey,' said Neville. He threw down the letter and put his arm around her. 'Come on, now.'

'I didn't want to worry you.'

'I know. Cheer up. It's not the end of

the world. I'll think of something.'

'You will?'

'Oh, yes. I've got a whole month to get something sorted out.'

'Yes,' said Gran, brightening up.

'That's true. You're a good lad, Neville. Where are you going?'

'Out into the garden. To have a think.'

'Don't you want your pie, dear?'

'Not right now. I'll save it for later.'

'All right. But put a muffler on. It's

chilly in the evenings.'

*   *   *

Outside, dusk was falling. A solitary owl flew across the darkening sky as Neville walked to the end of the tiny garden and flopped onto the ancient bench.

Plumtree Cottage stood in a forest clearing. There was a tumbledown fence, a vegetable patch, a well, a cucumber frame and a row of beehives. A couple of scrawny chickens clucked sleepily to each other in the hen house. To one side was a rickety old lean-to, which was Venetia's night quarters. He could hear her crashing about looking for carrots, completely unconcerned that the cart was broken and his life was in ruins.

The cottage itself was thatched, with roses growing over the door. It looked very pretty in the twilight, with soft light spilling from the kitchen window. You couldn't see the paint peeling from the door, or the rusty hinges on the bedroom shutters. It was home. He and

22

Gran had lived in it all their lives. Times had been hard, but at least they had always had a roof over their heads. Until now.

One hundred gold coins! His brain couldn't get around such an impossible sum.

Through the window he could see Gran pottering around, humming to herself as she cleared away the platters. Neville had said everything would be all right, and she believed him.

The circling owl landed in the tree above his head. It examined him with its head on one side, golden eyes gleaming. It opened its beak and hooted gently.

'*To do?*' it seemed to be saying. '*What are you to do?*'

For the life of him, he didn't know.

*　　　*　　　*

Three hours, two hedgehogs, some bats, a few moths and one inquisitive baby deer later, when the owl had long gone and all the stars were out, Neville came back in.

'Ah, there you are. I've saved the pie,' said Gran, who was in curlers.

'Lovely,' said Neville. 'I'll have it now, then.'

'Have you decided, dear? What you're going to do?' asked Gran, peering anxiously into his face.

'I have,' said Neville.

'What, then?'

Neville sat down and told her.

CHAPTER THREE

THE BEGGAR

'Seeking your fortune, eh?' said the friendly beggar. 'Well, that's . . . traditional.'

'I know,' said Neville. He nodded at the spotted cloth attached to a stick. 'I've got the bundle and everything.'

'So I see,' said the friendly beggar. 'Fine donkey, by the way.' He jerked a thumb at Venetia, who was ripping up the grass nearby.

'Yes,' agreed Neville. 'She's all right.

25

If you don't come up behind her unexpectedly.'

Neville had come across the friendly beggar sitting cross-legged beneath a signpost, where four roads met. He wore a battered top hat and a disgracefully patched overcoat. They had exchanged a few pleasantries about the weather, then the beggar had asked Neville for a penny and Neville had replied, truthfully, that he hadn't got one. The beggar hadn't seemed too put out and Neville had been riding since sun up, so he had decided to sit down and join him for a breather.

'What's in the bundle?' enquired the friendly beggar.

'Not much. A change of socks. Sandwiches.'

'Sandwiches, eh?' The beggar sounded wistful. 'What sort?'

'I don't know. Cucumber, probably. Would you like one?'

'Very kind of you, young sir, very kind!'

Neville untied the bundle and handed over a neat triangle. The beggar snatched it and downed it in one.

'Cor,' he said. 'That hit the spot, no trouble.' He held out a grimy hand. 'Hangdog Michael, that's me. Put it there, lad.'

'Pleased to meet you, Mr Hangdog,' said Neville. 'I'm Neville Niceguy.' He shook the hand, discreetly wiped his palm on his breeches, took out a boiled egg and sat back against the signpost. The sky was blue. The birds were singing. If it hadn't been for the pungent smell wafting from Hangdog Michael, everything would have been— well, not perfect, but not bad either.

'Youngest son, are we?' enquired Hangdog Michael, eyeing Neville's egg.

27

'No,' said Neville. 'There's just me and Gran. '

'It's usually the youngest son, see,' said Hangdog Michael. '*Traditionally* speakin'. The two older ones set out first an' meet a penniless beggar—like me for example—and refuse to share their last crust o' bread. An' terrible things befall 'em. Then the youngest 'as a turn, but 'e ain't a mean blighter like the other two, an' 'e gives away all 'is grub an' the beggar turns out to be a bootiful fairy in disguise an' 'e lives 'appily ever after.'

'Really?' said Neville. 'You're not a

fairy, by any chance?' he added hopefully.

'Well—no,' confessed Hangdog Michael. 'If I was, you wouldn't catch me 'angin' around wastin' me time with no youngest sons. I'd be off in fairyland, piggin' out on fairy cakes an' swiggin' back the nectar.'

'So you don't reckon much to begging, then? As a career?'

'Well, put it like this. It's not everyone can do it. You 'ave to get the *whine* right. You gotta make it so people feels guilty, but not so irritatin' that you gets on their nerves. I'll demonstrate.' He put on a tragic face and spoke in a mournful bleat, '*Good day, kind lady. You gotta kind face. Spare a penny for the poor old beggar man?* See?'

'You're not bad at it,' Neville complimented him.

'I know. I do all right, me. But I've 'ad a lot o' practice. If I was you, I'd try for something else.'

Neville smiled politely and took a bite of his egg. Hangdog Michael watched him like a hungry wolf. Neville couldn't stand it.

'Would you like a bit?' he asked.

'Would I!'

Neville handed it to him and Hangdog Michael fell upon it greedily.

'First decent bite I've 'ad in days,' he explained, chomping noisily.

'Oh dear. You can have the rest if you like.'

He regretted saying it almost before it was out of his mouth. It was the only food he had. Goodness knows where the next meal was coming from. But Gran always said that it never hurt to do a good turn and spread a little happiness around. And for a penniless beggar, Hangdog Michael certainly looked happy.

'Where are you off to, then?' asked Hangdog Michael, through a mouthful of sandwich.

Neville looked up at the signpost above their heads. One arm pointed north and read: *To the Mountains.* The second pointed west, and read: *To the Coast.* The third pointed east and read: *To the Town.* The fourth pointed south: *To The Forest*, back along the way he

30

had come.

'Which way would you suggest?' he asked.

'Depends on what you're lookin' for. Everybody's searching for somethin' different, right? Destiny. True Love. Adventure. The key to the outside toilet . . .'

'Oh, I know what I'm looking for,' said Neville. 'One hundred gold coins.'

Hangdog Michael gave a long whistle.

'That's an *awful* lot o' money,' he commented.

'I know. I need it in a hurry, too. We owe a lot of back rent, you see. Gran gave away our life savings, which didn't help.'

'Mmm,' said Hangdog Michael, and went all quiet. His eyes slid sideways to Neville's axe, which lay on the grass beside him.

'I s'pose you're a bit fed up about that?' he said casually, after a bit.

'Furious. If I came across the fellow she gave it to, I'd give him a piece of my mind, I can tell you. I don't suppose that's very likely, though. He'll be miles away by now.'

'Oh, sure to be. Miles and *miles.*'

'So we're completely broke, you see,' continued Neville. 'That's why I'm seeking my fortune. I suppose I should start by getting a job. Something that pays better than chopping trees.'

'Woodcutter, are we?' enquired Hangdog Michael, eyes still on the axe.

'Was,' said Neville, briefly. 'Not any more.

'What d'you need the axe for, then?'

'It's all I have. Apart from the clothes I'm standing up in. And the spare socks. Anyway, I thought it might come in useful as protection. In case I meet bears or something.'

'Ah.' For some reason, Hangdog Michael sounded relieved. 'Bears. Right.'

'I've never been to the mountains,' mused Neville. 'Or the sea, for that matter. But I'd probably stand a better chance of finding work in town. I'd flip a penny, if I had one to flip.'

Hangdog Michael pursed his lips. He seemed to be undergoing some sort of private struggle.

'I might 'ave a penny,' he said suddenly. 'One you can flip.'

'Really? I thought you were a penniless beggar.'

'Ah, but I'm a *successful* penniless beggar. That's the difference.'

He reached into his coat and withdrew a fat leather purse. Neville thought it looked rather well stuffed, for someone who claimed to be penniless. Hangdog Michael caught him looking and frowned. Politely, Neville looked the other way.

'Here,' said Hangdog Michael, after a moment. 'For you.' Neville thought he sounded rather smug. It probably made him feel good to hand out money instead of taking it for once.

'Thanks,' said Neville.

'You're most welcome,' said Hangdog Michael, graciously, raising his hat and giving a little bow.

'Right,' said Neville. 'Heads I go to the mountains, tails I go to the coast. Er—what shall I do about the town? I need a three sided coin.

'Ah, don't worry about it!' cried Hangdog Michael. 'Who needs to flip a coin anyway? Go to town. That's what you want to do, ain't it, young feller like you? The lights. The bustlin' crowds. The shops. The interestin' drainage system.'

'Yes,' confessed Neville. 'It is, really. We're a bit cut off, living in the forest. The farthest I've been is Little Mudwallop. That's the nearest village.

It's only got the one shop. I suppose town's quite jolly?'

'Can be,' said Hangdog Michael, guardedly. 'If you've got money to spend. Which I haven't. For example, I don't even have enough money to buy a new overcoat. Oh dear me no.'

'Oh, I shan't be buying anything. I must save every penny I earn. Yes, you're right. The town's my best bet. Here.'

He held out the penny. Hangdog Michael automatically reached out for it—then withdrew his hand. His face worked. He was obviously having another inner struggle. Finally, he said,

'That's all right. You keep it.'

'Oh, but I couldn't!' said Neville, shocked.

Taking money from a beggar! Whatever next?

'No, really,' said Hangdog Michael, rather grandly. He was obviously new to this generosity business. 'It's yours. One good turn deserves another, eh? Buy yourself a—bun or something.'

'Well—thanks,' said Neville. Carefully, he pocketed the penny, stood up, tucked his axe into his belt and began to retie his bundle back onto the stick. 'I'll be off, then. Nice meeting you, Mr Hangdog.'

'You too. Of course, if you do make your fortune and happen to come back this way, you could—er—return it? I don't want to seem mean, but you know. A penny's a penny.' Hangdog Michael's old ways died hard.

'I most certainly will,' agreed Neville, preparing to mount Venetia. ' 'Bye, then.'

'Good luck,' called his new friend. 'Watch out for yerself, you hear? There's a lot o' dishonest types in this world.'

'I will,' promised Neville. And with a wave, he rode off down the road with socks in his bundle, a penny in his pocket and a song in his heart.

Ten minutes later, he hauled on the reins and smacked his head sharply with the flat of his hand.

'Idiot!' he shouted. 'I'm an *idiot*!' Then he wheeled Venetia around and dug his heels into her sides. She gave an irritable snort, then broke into a lumbering trot.

They didn't stop until they reached the crossroads. Hangdog Michael, of course, had long gone.

CHAPTER FOUR

SPOT

'A bun, please,' said Neville, holding out his penny.

He had tried so hard not to spend his one and only precious coin, but he simply couldn't hold off any longer. He had spent the last hour walking around the cobbled market square being bombarded with sights, sounds and above all, *smells* which bypassed his brain and went straight to his stomach. Fragrant oranges, fat red tomatoes, sizzling sausages, roasted chestnuts, ripe cheeses—he'd never known anything like it.

Town was like nothing he had imagined in his wildest dreams. He had known it would be busy, but he wasn't prepared for *this*. This was *crazy*. Milkmaids, pie men, peddlers, onion sellers and shoeshine boys packed the streets, bellowing out their wares. Stout farmer's wives moved from stall to stall, poking at the fruit.

There were stalls selling colourful ribbons, bolts of cloth, shiny kettles, home-made toffee and 'cure-all' medicines in scary little black bottles. Cross looking chickens clucked in crates. Ragged urchins played noisy games of tag up curious little alleyways. Oh, it was wonderful! He couldn't believe he had lived all these years and not known that somewhere like this existed.

The woman on the baker's stall

handed him the bun, tossing his penny into a tin tray. It seemed rather a casual way to dispose of his entire fortune, but she wasn't to know. Neville wondered about asking her if she needed any help. Working on a bun stall would be a good job. But she had already turned away.

The bun looked nice, anyway. Sticky and fresh, with g l i s t e n i n g r a i s i n s . Venetia laid her head on his shoulder.

'Get off,' said Neville. 'This is mine.'

He opened his mouth to take a bite—and became aware of an u n p l e a s a n t s c r a t c h i n g sensation on his leg. He looked down. At his feet crouched a scruffy brown mongrel with a ludicrous mop head. Two bright eyes stared through the matted tangle. They were fixed unwaveringly on the bun. A long, pink, slavering tongue protruded below. Somewhere in amongst it all was a moist black nose.

'Hello, dog,' said Neville. 'What are you after, then?'

The dog whimpered and put its shaggy head on one side. Its stumpy tail gave a little wag. It lifted a paw and left it dangling sweetly in mid air. The eyes never left the bun.

'Want a bit?' said Neville. 'Here.' He broke off a piece and held it out.

'*Rrrrrrrrrumph!*'

The head shot forward, the jaws gaped—and it was gone. Neville snatched his hand away and counted his fingers.

'My word,' he said. 'You're a hungry little chap, no mistake. 'Bye, then.'

He ruffled the dog's head, turned and moved away, tugging Venetia behind him. He passed a flower stall, an old boots stall, and paused to examine one selling spectacularly ugly china vases. He opened his mouth to take a bite of bun. Again, he felt scratching on his leg.

He looked down. The dog was grinning up at him, unwavering eyes riveted on the bun.

'You again?' said Neville. Up came the paw. 'Sorry, that's your lot. This is my supper, see. Off you go. Home, boy.'

'Ain't got no 'ome. It's a stray, that one,' the stall owner told him. He was a surly looking man with a lot of black teeth. 'Always hangin' around on the scrounge. Give it a kick.'

'I don't believe in kicking animals,' Neville told him, sharply. 'You have to be firm, but kind. That's much the best way.' He looked over at the man's vases. 'Anyway, it wouldn't want to scrounge any of your vases. I bet you have trouble *giving* those away.' He looked down. 'Stay! And that's an order. Good dog. You see?'

And with a curt nod to the stall holder, he moved on. When he had gone a short way, he risked a quick look back over his shoulder. There was no sign of the dog.

'You see, Venetia? Firm but kind, that's the way, eh?' he said. He turned and immediately tripped over something furry in the way of his feet. He landed painfully on his knees on the rubbish strewn cobblestones and found himself inches away from a familiar pair of eyes. Above him, Venetia lowered her head and looked for carrots in his hair.

'Look,' said Neville, exasperated, as

the knees of passers-by buffeted his
head. 'I've told you . . .'

He broke off. The dog was holding
something clamped between its jaws.
Something small, thick and square. It
looked like a pocket book.

'What have you got there?' said
Neville. He reached out and took hold
of the book. The dog's jaws remained
firmly clamped. It gave a playful little
growl deep in its throat and braced its
legs, all set for a jolly game of tug-o'-

war.

'Come on, let go. Let go, I say. Drop it, there's a good . . . oh, all *right!*' He placed the last of his bun on the cobbles.

'*Rrrrrmmmmmmmffff!*'

The book dropped into his hand as the dog fell upon the morsel.

Neville climbed to his feet, rubbed his sore knees, took Venetia's bridle and limped over to an empty packing crate by a wall. Gratefully, he flopped down and examined the book. It had a leather cover, currently rather soggy and pitted with teeth marks. He opened it at random. The pages were covered with spidery writing, interspersed with odd diagrams and meaningless rows of figures. Venetia peered helpfully over his shoulder.

'Stop it,' Neville told her, pushing her away. 'Does this look like a carrot? Get your teeth out of my face.'

He found what he was looking for on the inside cover. In the same spidery writing, it said:

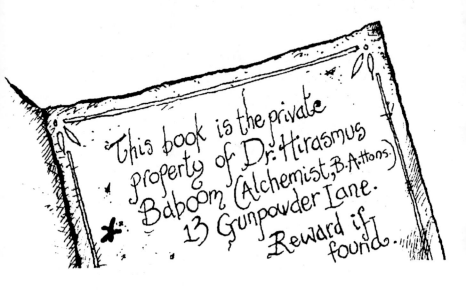

This book is the private property of Dr. Hirasmus Baboom (Alchemist, B.Attons.) 13 Gunpowder Lane. Reward if found.

Reward, eh? Of course, Gran would say that the *real* reward came from doing a good deed. Still, a penny or two would come in handy.

Just then, a heavy paw plonked on his lap. The dog was sitting at his feet, gazing up into his face. Neville reached down and tugged its ears.

'Seems like destiny's thrown us together, boy,' he said. 'Is that what you want? To come along with me and be my dog?' Clouds of dust rose as he ruffled its fur. 'Well, that's all right by me. What shall I call you, eh? How about Spot? I've always wanted a dog called Spot. How about that?'

'Whuff,' said Spot, intelligently.

'Hey, Spot! Attaboy, Spot! Just wait

'til we get home. You're going to love the woods.'

Wincing slightly, he stood up. Spot shot to his feet, panting excitedly.

'Come on, then,' said Neville. 'We'd better return this to its rightful owner. Oh, it's going to be *great*, having you along as my faithful companion. There's nothing like a dog's loyalty. The way might be long and hard, but we'll have each other, won't we? So what if I don't have a bean? So what if we go hungry? So what if . . . Spot?'

The dog had turned and was briskly trotting away.

'Spot?' shouted Neville. 'Come back! Where are you going?'

The dog didn't even pause. The last Neville saw of him was a stubby tail disappearing into the distance.

Neville felt terribly hurt. For a few minutes there, he had been a dog owner. It had felt good. Now it was all over.

'Was it the name, d'you think?' he asked Venetia. Sighing deeply, he tugged on her bridle and they moved on.

CHAPTER FIVE

THE ALCHEMIST

It took a while to find Gunpowder Street, despite being given detailed directions by a deaf old lady with a walking stick. She had reeled off a whole string of instructions regarding right turns, left turns and bits where you just followed your nose. The town was a maze of confusing, identical cobbled streets lined with identical houses, interspersed with rather sinister looking alleyways. When Neville finally found himself standing on the doorstep of Number Thirteen, both he and Venetia had had more than enough.

Number Thirteen differed from all the other houses in the road. There was a large, gaping hole in the roof, all the windows were boarded up and the front door was badly charred.

At some point in the not too distant past, it had clearly been the scene of a rather large explosion. There was a blackened plaque hanging sideways from a single nail. It read:

Dr. Hirasmus Baboom
(B.A. hons)
Alchemist
Beware of EXPLOSIONS!

Neville wasn't too sure what an alchemist actually *did*. He had a vague idea that it might be something to do with the dispensing of coloured pills, perfumed soaps and novelty hot water bottle covers, but the state of the building didn't quite fit.

He stuck his axe into the special loop on Venetia's saddle. Gran always said it wasn't polite to take an axe indoors. He kept hold of his bundle, though. He was darned if he was going to be parted from his spare socks. He pulled on the bell rope and waited. After a moment, there came the sound of footsteps and an irritable voice cried out:

'Jah? Who is zis?'

'Dr Baboom?' enquired Neville. 'Dr *Hirasmus* Baboom?'

'Jah, jah. Who is it vants him? If you are a doorstep salesman, forget it. I haff enough inferior oven gloves and cheap dish mops to start a shop.'

'I'm not a salesman.'

'Vot, zen? A spy? Come to vinkle out my secrets?' The voice was dark with suspicion.

'No,' said Neville, patiently. 'Not a

spy. Look, my name's Neville . . .'

'I don't like it. Go avay.'

'But I found something in the market that belongs to you, sir. A notebook.'

There was a long pause, followed by the sound of rattling chains. The door swung open and Dr Baboom stood before him.

He was small and thin, with masses of wild grey hair which seemed to sprout s t r a i g h t upwards, like a n c i e n t mustard and cress grown in an egg shell. He wore a pair of half-glasses which made his pinkish eyes seem bigger at the bottom. He sported a

scorched, stained robe. His fingers were covered in bandages and he had no eyebrows. Dr Baboom looked as though he played with fire a lot.

'My book? You haff found my book? May ze elements be praised!' He reached out and snatched the book from Neville's hand. 'Come in, my boy, come in!'

Neville attached Venetia's bridle to the hitching ring in the wall, patted her nose and followed the odd little man inside.

He found himself in a long, dark passageway. It felt uncomfortably warm. The doctor skipped ahead of him, muttering, 'My book! Ze honest boy has found my book!' in a joyful way.

Then:

'In you come!' he announced. 'Velcome to my humble lab, honest boy!' And he threw open a door.

It was like opening the door of an oven. The heat rushed out, hitting Neville smack in the face. He gasped and staggered back. It was the kind of heat that made you want to lie at the

bottom of a pond, breathing through a straw. He could almost feel his skin peeling.

'Is a little stuffy,' apologised the doctor, bouncing along behind. 'But ve alchemists are used to zat.'

The laboratory was pretty well devoted to fire. An enormous fireplace was set in the wall at one end, putting out the kind of heat that normally issues from a furnace. A massive

cauldron hung over it on a chain. Glowing braziers were dotted around the room. Lead bowls full of yellow liquid bubbled on the top. Candles flared. Smoke billowed.

There were barrels set around the sooty walls. Some were dangerously close to the braziers. They had chalked labels reading *ROCKS* and *MORE ROCKS* and—alarmingly— *GUNPOWDER.*

A bench ran down one side containing various glass test tubes, flasks and crucibles, all connected up with complicated rubber tubing. An open bottle marked POISON stood amongst a large collection of dirty mugs and a plateful of dry biscuits. A large iron pump stood at one end of the room. It had a handle at one side, and a bucket stood beneath the spout.

'Wow!' wheezed Neville, through a sandpaper throat. 'It's certainly hot.'

'Vot can I get you? A nice cup of scalding hot tea? A cup of hot chocolate, perhaps?' The doctor was tripping over himself in his anxiety to be hospitable. Narrowly avoiding a brazier, he scuttled to the bench and began crashing about with mugs. His sleeve brushed across a candle and caught alight.

'Bozzer!' he cried, dancing around and blowing out the flames. 'Alvays zat happens!'

'A glass of water, please,' rasped Neville, hastily.

The doctor seized a mug, scurried to a stone sink in the corner and turned on the tap. Beaming, he thrust it at Neville.

'Zere! Drink, my boy. You haff earned it. So long I haff searched for my book. I confess I had given up hope. It contains important notes plus many secret formulae, vital to my experiments. I am most grateful, lad. A dry biscuit?'

'Er—not just yet.'

Neville swallowed a mouthful of tepid water and fanned himself with his hat. The doctor watched him, nodding encouragingly.

'Well,' said Neville, trying to be as polite as you can be when roasting alive. 'This is all very—interesting. What are you doing exactly, sir?'

'Aha.' The doctor lowered his voice and sidled up. 'Vot you see before you,' he explained, thrillingly, 'is my Great Vurk.'

Neville looked around. He wondered what a Vurk was. Perhaps it was the big metal pump thing in the corner.

'I mean,' said the doctor, seeing Neville's puzzled expression, 'by zat I mean my latest, greatest experiment. Are you versed in ze skills of alchemy, lad?'

'Well—no. Actually, I don't really know what an alchemist does,' confessed Neville. 'We don't have them where I come from.'

'No? Vot *do* you haff vere you come from?'

'Trees, mainly.'

'I see. A simple country boy. Viz a bundle on a stick. You vouldn't haff a sandvich in zere, by any . . . ?'

'No,' said Neville. 'Sorry.'

'No matter, no matter. So. Zere are

60

no *alchemists* in your neck of ze voods? No vizards, sorcerers, miracle vorkers or such like?'

'Not as far as I know. We had a gypsy palmist at the village fayre once. She said there was a lot of luck coming my way. I tripped over a tent peg on the way out and sprained my toe. I don't think she was much good.'

'Palmists! Ha!' Doctor Baboom waved a dismissive hand. 'Can a *palmist* discover ze Philosopher's Stone? Can a *palmist* create ze Elixir of Life?'

'I don't know. Why? Can you?' asked Neville, interested.

'Vell—no,' admitted Dr Baboom. 'Not yet. Zey are difficult. Zey both require ze addition of gunpowder, you see. I confess I am heavy handed viz ze gunpowder. But who cares? Who needs ze boring old Philosopher's Stone? Who cares about ze over-rated Elixir of Life? Not me! Not ven I haff made ze greatest breakthrough in ze history of alchemy!'

'What's that, then?' enquired Neville, peering around at the bubbling bowls of yellow stuff and the mass of complicated equipment.

Dr Baboom reached out a skinny arm and pulled Neville close.

'Tell me, boy. Can I trust you? Can you keep a secret?'

'Certainly I can,' said Neville, rather offended. 'Gran didn't bring me up to be a tattle-tale. Thanks for the water. I think I should go now.'

'Hey, hey! Don't get on your high

donkey! I just needed to be sure. Forgive me. I trust you. And because I trust you, I vill tell you. Better still, I vill *show* you! Go over to ze Goldometer.'

'The . . . ?'

'Ze big pump over zere. Zat's ze vun. Now zen. Pull ze handle.'

Neville did as he was told. From somewhere deep within came a grinding noise. Then from the spout streamed a steady, glittering stream of . . .

'Gold coins,' said Neville in choked tones as they rained down into the bucket. 'Dozens of 'em.'

'Hundreds,' said the doctor, airily.

'Thousands, even. Yes, my boy. I, Hirasmus Baboom, *haff discovered how to make rocks into gold!*'

'Wow!' breathed Neville. 'How?'

'Oh, I can't possibly explain *zat*. You need a brain ze size of a planet to understand zat. I see you are impressed.'

'I am,' said Neville, staring down into the gleaming bucket. 'Very impressed. So—er—how many coins to a bucket,

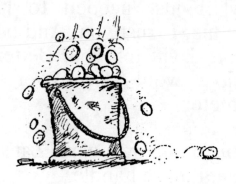

would you say?'

'Boy, zere is enough gold in zere to purchase a small kingdom—and plenty more vere zat came from. Oh, yes. I am rich beyond your vildest dreams. Of course, I am not interested in ze money. It is knowing zat I am a genius zat counts. Vot do I vant viz *money*? I vill probably give it all avay to deserving causes. But enough of me. You vill be vanting to get along. Are you sure you won't haff a biscuit?'

'I'll take one for later, please,' said Neville.

'Take two. Is zere anysing else you require? Anysing at all?'

'We . . . ell,' said Neville, his eyes returning to the overflowing bucket. 'Now you come to mention it . . .'

CHAPTER SIX

SPOT AGAIN

'*We're in the money!*' sang Neville, as he rode along the cobbled street. 'Oh, I can't believe it, Venetia! It was so easy! I've got the hundred coins, plus ten more for luck!' Cheerfully, he waved the clinking sack. 'So we'll go back to the market and get treats. A pie for me, a carrot for you and something nice for Gran. Then we'll have a slap-up meal at an inn before setting off for home. My, will Gran be pleased to see us! Oh, I simply can't believe it was that *easy*!'

Back in the market square, there was no sign of the crowds dwindling, although it was getting late. The stall holders were still doing brisk business by torchlight. The pie man still hawked his wares. The bun lady still had a long queue. The ugly vase salesman, Neville was pleased to note, still had no customers. It seemed that the market square was the hub of all night life in the town.

A sturdy man in official looking chainmail was standing by a hot mead stall, slurping from a tin mug. A stout

cudgel swung from his belt. This must be a night watchman.

Neville had never seen one before. There wasn't a great call for night watchmen in Fingle Forest.

'Good evening, officer,' he said, and saluted respectfully. 'Great outfit, by the way. Very smart.'

The watchman's suspicious little eyes bored into him, hoping to find evidence of sarcasm. But all he saw was Neville's cheery, open face. He grunted and turned his back.

Feeling more confident, now that he was a man of means, Neville dismounted and moved along the stalls. He was looking for something suitable for Gran. She didn't get out much these days. She'd like a present from faraway places. What, though?

His eye alighted on a stall selling hand-painted picture postcards. Very pretty, some of them were, with thatched cottages, fluffy ducks and kittens. The one that caught his eye, though, was a picture of *the very marketplace in which he was now standing!* The artist had a real eye for detail. It showed the pie man, the milkmaids and everything! There was even the bun stall! What could be a better souvenir? Gran would be thrilled. Particularly when he pointed to it and grandly announced: *'And I stood there.'*

'How much?' he asked the stall holder—a ferrety man with a droopy moustache.

'Twopence,' said the man.

'I haven't got anything small, I'm afraid,' apologised Neville. He rummaged in his sack, took out a gold coin and placed it in the stall holder's palm. The man stared down at it, eyes bulging.

'What's this?' he said. 'You expect me to have change for *this*?'

'Well—yes. Don't you?'

The man looked up, suddenly deeply suspicious.

'Where did you get this? Who'd you rob?'

'I didn't rob *anybody*. I was given it as a reward, if you must know.'

'Oh yeah?' said the man. He might as well have said '*Liar!*' The meaning was the same.

Neville reached out and removed the coin from the man's hand. 'It seems you don't want my money,' he said, stiffly. 'Well, that's just fine by me.'

' 'Old it,' said the man 'Not so fast. Let's 'ave another look at that.'

'Too late,' said Neville. 'You'll not have my custom today, that's for sure.'

He clicked to Venetia and stalked off. A few yards further on, he bumped into the pie man, who had one solitary pie left.

'I'll have that,' said Neville, pointing. 'Please.'

' 'Tiz a bit squashed, son,' said the pie man, looking at the flattened slab of pastry with brown slime oozing from the edges. 'I was about to sling it,

69

actually.'

'I'll still have it,' said Neville. 'Thank you for your honesty. Here. Keep the change. I've had a bit of luck today.'

Generously, he pressed the gold coin into the pie man's hand and walked on, leaving him open-mouthed and staring at his palm in disbelief.

Eagerly, Neville raised the pie to his lips and took a deep, satisfying bite. Squashed, it was—but by now he was so hungry he could have eaten his own shoes.

There was a scratching at his calf. He hardly dared look. Was it possible? Could it really be . . . ?

YES! IT WAS!

'Spot.' he bellowed. 'Look, Venetia! It's good old *Spot*! Where have you *been*, boy? Why did you go off to like that? Never mind, it's great to see you. Here, have some pie!'

'*Rrrrrrrmmmmmmmmmmfffffff!*'

'Hey, that really hit the spot, didn't it? Hey, hear what I said? I said, hit the *Spot*, ha ha!'

Spot flung himself onto his back and wriggled, paws paddling the air, awash with love and devotion. Neville crouched down and tickled his tummy.

'Oh, *Spot*!' he said, fondly. 'Now we can really be a proper family again. Know what I'm going to do? I'm going to get you a lead, so that you don't wander off and get lost again. Proper dogs have leads. I saw a rope stall around here somewhere. Come on, boy, let's go!'

*　　　*　　　*

The rope stall was minded by a bored young girl with untidy hair pulled back with a piece of string. Great, hairy coils of rope were piled before her. Loops of it hung like tree snakes from the tarpaulin over her head.

'Money for ole rope, mister?' she asked, seeing Neville looking.

'Yes. I'll have a length for my dog, please. That coil over there looks about right. Can I try it on him?'

'Suit yerself.'

She folded her arms and stared as

Neville crouched down and attached the rope around his new pet's head. Spot put his paws on Neville's shoulders and lovingly licked his nose.

'How's that, boy? Not too tight?' He smiled up at the girl. 'He's called Spot.'

The girl flicked disinterested eyes over Spot, who was trying to stare at his own neck in a puzzled way. ' 'E aint got a spot,' she said.

'I know. But, you see, I've always wanted a dog called Spot. How much do I owe?'

'Three pennies.'

Neville rummaged in his sack, fished out another gold coin and held it out. The girl stared.

'What's up?' said Neville. 'Don't you have any change?'

'Not for that, I don't,' said the girl, with an odd look in her eyes. 'I'll 'ave to get my dad.'

'Oh, look, never mind. Keep it.' Cheerfully, he tossed the coin on the counter. 'I'm in the money, as it happens. My gran always says you should share your good fortune. But perhaps you could do me a favour. I've got a long walk ahead of me tonight. I'm going home, you see. But first, I'm going to treat myself to a slap-up meal. Can you direct me to a good inn? Somewhere jolly, with a bit of an atmosphere?'

'There's the Spud and Maggot,' said the girl, slowly. Her eyes never left the gold coin, but she made no move to pick it up. 'Down the alley, over the bridge, on the right.'

'Thanks,' said Neville. 'Well, good evening to you, Miss.'

The girl watched him go, whistling jauntily as he went. As soon as he was out of sight, she snatched up the coin, bit down deeply on it and studied it for a moment. Then:

'Pa!' she shouted. 'Come 'ere a minute! I got summint ter show yer!'

CHAPTER SEVEN

THE SPUD AND MAGGOT

'Yes?' said the landlord of the Spud and Maggot, wiping his hands on a greasy cloth, then drawing one across his nose, which was running.

'Good evening, landlord,' said Neville, pleasantly. 'A pint of your best milk. Don't spare the cream.'

'No milk,' said the landlord. 'Just beer.'

'Oh. Right. Beer, then.'

The landlord pulled a pint in silence and pushed it across to Neville.

'Anythin' else?'

'Well, yes. I'm after a hot meal. What can you offer?'

'An 'ot spud,' said the landlord, pointing to a chalked notice. It read:

'Uh huh. And what else?'

There was a short pause while the landlord stared at him.

'Another 'ot spud?' he ventured, at length.

'I see,' said Neville. 'And what's for pudding?'

'Well, now,' said the landlord. 'Let me think.' He scratched his head thoughtfully. ' 'Ot spud and treacle?'

'Ha, ha,' chortled Neville. 'Spoiled for choice, eh? Well, you know, perhaps I'll settle for the potato.'

'One or two?'

'Two. I'm celebrating.'

The landlord reached up and pulled on the rope of a bell which hung over his head.

'TWO SPUDS, BESSIE!' he bellowed. Then placed his elbows on the greasy counter and picked at his teeth with a fork.

'Fine place you've got here,' said Neville, looking around at the greasy, sawdust strewn floor, the yellowed walls and the solitary old man who sat hunched over a foaming tankard in a shadowy corner. He had never been into an inn before. This would be another exciting experience to tell Gran all about. It wasn't quite the hive of jollity that he had hoped for, but he could use a bit of poetic licence.

The old man in the corner was staring at him. Neville gave him a friendly little wave. The old man looked away and stared back into his pint. A door opened and a sour-faced woman bustled out with a plate containing a hot potato, which she slammed down on the table.

'There you go, Sid,' she said. 'One 'ot spud. That'll be a shillin'.'

'My word!' said Neville. 'That smells good!' The landlord carried on picking at his teeth. The woman scooped up a coin and banged back through the door without even looking at him. It really wasn't a very friendly place.

Neville raised his tankard to his lips. He'd never tasted beer before. He took a sip, choked, and hastily put it down, making a mental note never to taste it again. Suddenly, he thought of something.

'Excuse me, landlord. I wonder if I

might trouble you for a bone for my dog?'

'What dog?' said the landlord.

'Why, Spot here,' said Neville. He looked down at the empty space by his feet. 'That's funny. He was here a moment ago.'

'Do you mean *that* dog?' said the landlord, nodding his head towards the old man in the corner. Neville looked. Spot was camped by the old man's ankles, paw dangling sweetly in mid air and ears perked in winsome begging pose.

'That's him,' said Neville, relieved.

'That's the stray that 'angs around the market. What d'you want *'im* for? Anyway, he don't 'ave a spot,' said the landlord.

'I know. But he's mine now and I've always wanted a dog called Spot. Hey! Spot! Over here, boy.'

Spot ignored him. His head was slowly moving upwards, pulled by an invisible string as the old man raised a trembling spoonful of potato to his lips.

'We're huge friends already,' Neville told the landlord. 'Aren't we, Spot?' He

gave a little whistle and patted his
knees vigorously. 'Come on, Spot.
Heel, boy!'

Spot's response was to lay his head
on the old man's bony knee. Just then,
a serving hatch opened behind the bar
and an arm appeared and banged down
a plate on the ledge. The landlord

picked it up, using his greasy cloth.

'Mine? Ooh, lovely!' said Neville, looking around in vain for a napkin to tuck into his shirt or, at the very least, a fork. He reached out his hand and grasped the plate.

'That'll be a shillin,' said the landlord, holding on.

'Oh. Right.' Neville reached down and swung his sack of gold coins onto the counter. They landed with a satisfying thump. 'I'm afraid I haven't got anything small,' he began. 'I hope you've got some cha . . .'

The inn door flew open with a crash. The landlord jumped. The hot potatoes fell off the plate and rolled across the floor to Spot, who ate them in a couple of mouthfuls.

'What the . . . ?'

'Hold it right there, boy!' ordered a voice. 'Don't you move a muscle!'

Neville whirled around. Standing in the doorway, cudgel at the ready and face puffed with importance, was the night watchman from the market place. Behind him, craning over his shoulder, were the man from the postcard stall,

83

the pie man and the rope girl. Neville got another of his *bad* feelings.

'That's 'im!' cried the rope girl. 'That's 'im what's been passin' the forged coins!'

'Caught in the act, no less!' chimed in the postcard man.

'Go on, officer—arrest 'im!' urged the pie man, eagerly.

'What?' squeaked Neville. 'But I— what makes you think—I never . . . *forged*?'

'Forged,' nodded the night watchman grimly, striding forward. 'And don't try tellin' me you never knowed.'

'Well I'm jiggered!' said the landlord. 'You artful little swindler, you! After all my 'ospitality!'

'But I—look, stop doing that, will you? Take that stick out of my back, or I warn you, my dog will—ouch—Spot! Where are you, boy? Look, this is all a mistake . . . Spoooottt . . .'

Still shouting, he was frogmarched out into the night.

CHAPTER EIGHT

JAIL

'But I haven't *done* anything, I tell you!' Neville shouted through the bars.

'Now, where have I heard *that* before?' said the warder. He was leaning against the wall opposite, idly tossing Neville's cell key from one hand to the other. 'Wait a minute! Of course! It was the prisoner *before you*! Oh, yeah, and the one *before 'im*! I *knew* I'd 'eard it somewhere.'

Neville had always imagined prison warders as huge, gloating brutes in leather jerkins with knuckles which brush the floor. This warder, in contrast, was thin and miserable, with a long, wandering nose and a nasty line in sarcasm.

'For the last time, I didn't *steal* it!'

'Oh, we know *that*,' the warder informed him. 'You ain't charged with robbery.'

'What, then?'

'Passin' fake money, innit?' He nodded at the sack of gold coins which lay on a small table. It now bore a small label marked *Eviduns.* 'Serious crime, that,' he added.

'But—look, those coins *aren't* fake! They're real!'

'Oh yeah?' The warder reached into the sack, withdrew a coin and bit down on it. 'See? Teef marks, innit?'

'But Dr Baboom *assured* me that . . .'

'Aha. Baboom eh?' the Warder nodded sagely. 'Say no more. He's been up to his tricks again, has he?'

'Yes, Yes! You know of him? Dr Hirasmus Baboom, 13 Gunpowd . . . what? What tricks?'

The Warder sighed. 'Country boy, are we? Straight from the woods? Wet behind the ears? Not used to the wicked ways of town?'

'Well—yes, but . . . ?'

'Thought so. You never learn, you lads.' The warder shook his head. 'You been taken for a ride, son. Well known hereabouts is our Dr Baboom. Or should I say'—he paused for dramatic effect—' . . . Barkin' Bert!'

'Barkin who?'

'Bert. That's his real name, innit? Bert Parkin. Everyone calls him Barkin' Bert Parkin. Used to run the night cart, collectin' all the rubbish and the you-know-what. By that, I mean . . .'

'All right, all right, I know what you mean,' said Neville, hastily.

'Right. Anyway, Bert goes and finds an old book about chemistry in the dustbin, innit? Decides he'll have a change of life and next thing you know, he's sent away fer some some test tubes and what-not, and puttin' on a daft accent and calling himself Dr Hirasmus Baboom. Starts sendin' letters to the paper claimin' he's sorted out the secrets o' the universe. Alchemist? Don't make me laugh. If he's an alchemist, I'm the Fairy Queen ...'

He suddenly broke off. From somewhere up above, there came the distant sound of trampling feet and raised voices, topped with an almighty bellowing, like an enraged bull.

' 'Ang about. Duty calls, innit?'

'You can leave the key with me if you like,' offered Neville helpfully. But the warder's footsteps were already receding up the stone steps.

Neville sat down on the bunk and put his head in his hands. So the gold wasn't real after all. He might have known life wasn't that simple. He'd done someone a favour and that was the thanks he got. How could he have been so stupid?

But he hadn't known, had he? It wasn't his fault that Dr Baboom had turned out to be a mad bin man with delusions of grandeur. Surely they would let him go, when he explained everything? Yes, of course they would. On the other hand, it might be a good idea to work out a plan of escape. Just in case.

He raised his head and stared around the cell. Three paces long and three wide. Narrow bunk, bars at the front, thick stone walls on the other three sides. There was a small, high, barred window that opened at gutter level onto the street above. If he stood on tiptoe he could just see the feet of passers-by. That was all. No useful trapdoor down to the sewers or loose brick leading to an escape passage. Not that he would need to escape when he explained everything, of course. They didn't have a thing on him. Not a thing.

He stood up and stretched. It was then that something fell from inside his jerkin. It was the picture postcard! He'd just walked off with it, quite forgetting to pay! Oh well. Too late now. At least he could try getting a message to Gran. He didn't want her to worry. Perhaps the warder would be kind enough to post it for him, if he asked politely. He scrabbled in his pocket, finally located a pencil stub, balanced the card on his knee, stuck out his tongue and began to write.

Shortly, there came the sound of footsteps descending the stairs. The angry roaring was getting louder. The warder was returning—with company.

'Here we are again, then,' came the warder's voice. 'Couple of little chums for you, innit? In case you're feeling lonely.'

The key rattled in the lock, the door opened—and all of a sudden, the cell was a whole lot more crowded.

CHAPTER NINE

CELL MATES

'In you go, boys. You can cool off in there for a bit,' said the warder. He turned to the watchmen who had accompanied him down. 'Right, officers, you can leave 'em to me. I'll see you out.'

All three vanished up the stone steps to the regions above, leaving Neville alone with his new cell mates. He wasn't at all keen on what he saw.

Both men were dressed in exceedingly smelly, dirty sheepskins. One was short and skinny, with gold rings in his ears, a filthy bandana wound around his head and a sharp, crafty face. The other was enormous. His head was shaven, apart from a greasy pigtail which sprouted from the back. He had hands like hams, a body like a wardrobe and tree trunk legs ending in huge furry boots. He was

currently rattling at the bars and
bellowing at the top of his voice.

'URURURURURUUUUUUUUR!'

'Pipe down, Burk, will ya?' said the
skinny one. 'They've gone, doncha see?
Besides, you're deafenin' the kid 'ere.'

'UR?'

Slowly, the big one turned around.
His small, close-set eyes alighted on
Neville.

'That's all right,' said Neville, hastily.
'Don't mind me. You carry on.'

'URUR?'

'He says you can carry on, Burk. But
I reckon he's just bein' polite.' He

winked and stuck out a grimy hand. 'Ratsy's the name, kid. This 'ere's Burk the Berserker.'

'Neville Niceguy,' said Neville, taking the leathery palm. 'Pleased to meet you, Ratsy.'

'Likewise, Nev.'

'Actually it's Neville,' began Neville, then stopped. Actually, Nev was all right, shorter, sharper, more action-packed, less . . . square. He liked it. From now on, he would be Nev.

'Well, it shouldn't be. Trust me, son. The Neville Niceguys of this world never get nowhere. To me, you'll always be Nev. What you in for, Nev?'

'Passing fake money,' admitted Nev, shamefacedly. He was about to go on to explain that it was all a terrible mistake, but he didn't get the chance.

'Hear that, Burk?' Ratsy was looking at him with admiration. 'The kid's been runnin' the old dodgy coins scam! Never think it to look at 'im, would yer? I take it that's what in the sack over there?'

'Yes, but . . .'

'Well, well. I 'ad you down for a

simple country lad, Nev, what with the bundle and that. I don't suppose . . . ?'

'No,' said Neville. 'No sandwiches. Just socks.'

'Pity. It's a while since we 'ad a square meal, eh, Burk?'

'URURURURURURUR!' bellowed Burk, charging the wall and butting it with his head. A large chunk of plaster fell away.

'What's he doing?' asked Nev, with a wince.

'Berserkin',' said Ratsy, with a shrug. ' 'E's a Berserker. That's what they do. Gets on yer nerves, don't it? Burk, I told you to give it a rest. Down, boy.'

'So,' said Nev. 'What—er—brings you here, Ratsy?'

'Bit of a scene in the tavern. Burk 'ere carelessly broke a chair.'

'Gosh,' said Nev. 'They arrested you for that?'

'It was over the landlord's head,' explained Ratsy, with a grin.

'Oh. I see. Er—what tavern would that be, then?'

'The Crossed Axes. Over in Union Street. 'Eck of a ruckus, it were. Glasses flyin', folks screamin'. Lovely. Took six of 'em to bring us down, didn't it, Burk?'

'UR,' agreed Burk, proudly.

'Sounds a bit more lively than the Spud and Maggot,' said Nev, somewhat wistfully.

'Oh, yeah. The Spud's a dump. Nobody goes there. Nothin' to nick. The Axes is the place. Lovely big till they got there, chock full o' dosh, just ripe for the takin'.'

'Is that what you were doing?' asked Nev, with a little gulp. 'Robbing the till?'

' 'Course. We likes robbin' tills, don't

we, Burk? The change does us good.'

Just then, the warder returned. Burk threw himself at the bars again.

'URURURURURURURUR!'

'Now, now. Don't try to get round me with your soft words,' said the warder. He had a large, rolled-up piece of paper under his arm. He turned his back and proceeded to stick it to the wall opposite the cell.

'Oi! Warder! Is that your nose, or are you eatin' a banana?' jeered Ratsy.

'Funny man, eh? Well, you won't be laughing when you see the judge. There.' The warder stood back and inspected his handiwork. 'Thought you boys might like a pretty picture to brighten your pitiful lives.'

It was a 'wanted poster'. The face that stared out was badly drawn, horribly smudged and topped with wild corkscrews of hair. It looked liked a child's chalk drawing. Below were the words:

Wanted, Dead or Alive!

Big Ma Manky, Leader of the notorious gang of thieving cut throat desperados known as - The Mountain Boys.

Reward if captured — ONE HUNDRED GOLD COINS.

'URURURURURURURUR!'
Burk rattled the bars with renewed frenzy.

'All right, Burk, calm down,' said Ratsy, reaching up and patting his elbow. 'Hey, warder. Are we eatin' out tonight? I don't smell nothin' burnin'.'

'Oh, *funny*. I'll 'ave to go and sit down I'm laughin' so hard, innit?'

'Excuse me,' said Nev, humbly.

'What now?' said the warder.

'I'm worried about my dog and my donkey. Is someone taking care of them?'

'How should I know? Got enough worries with the animals down here, innit?'

And with that, he turned and vanished up the steps.

'Small, grey donkey, was it? Sulky lookin'?' enquired Ratsy.

'That's right! That's Venetia. Why, have you . . . ?'

'Tethered outside. Saw it when we come in. Didn't see no dog with a spot, though.'

'He hasn't got a spot.'

'Why'd you call him Spot, then?'

'Because I've always wanted a dog called Spot. Oh, I hope he's all right.' With a sigh, Nev returned to his postcard.

'What's that yer doin', Nev?' enquired Ratsy, peering over his shoulder.

'I'm writing to my gran,' explained Nev.

'No kiddin'! See that, Burk? Young Nev 'ere can write. Very useful skill that.'

'Yes, well, I don't want her to worry. I hope I'm not going to be stuck in here for long.'

'No tellin',' said Ratsy. 'Could be days. Weeks, even.'

'*What?* But I've only got a month to get the money!'

'What money might that be, then, Nev?' enquired Ratsy, sounding interested.

'One hundred gold coins. We're being evicted. We owe it to the old Squire. I have to get it somehow. There's *got* to be a way.'

'There is,' said Ratsy. 'Nick it. That's what I'd do.'

'Oh, I don't believe in stealing. No, there are better ways than that. I can work hard and save, and . . .'

'. . . and maybe, in ten years, you'll have enough,' said Ratsy. 'Think again, kid. Use yer brains. Now, if only you could think of a way of gettin' us out of 'ere, you could try fobbin' off that there sack o' fake coins on the Squire. He's an old geezer, you say? Probably short-sighted. Chances are 'e's too dozy to know the difference.'

'I couldn't do that either!' cried Nev, shocked. 'That'd be dishonest.'

'Might work, though,' said Ratsy, slyly.

Nev's eyes followed Ratsy's to the unattended sack on the table. Ratsy was right. It might work. The Old Squire was getting on in years. He probably wouldn't even try spending it—just stick it in a cupboard somewhere . . . No. He pulled himself up. Mustn't think like that.

'No,' he said firmly. 'Gran wouldn't like it.

'Poor old soul won't like bein' made 'omeless either. You got to do somethin'.'

'I know. I know! I will! I'll come up with a plan. I'll . . . I'll . . .' Nev cast about wildly for another money-making scheme. His anxious eyes alighted on the poster that the warder had displayed for their pleasure. He pointed.

'Look! See that? The Mountain Boys. They sound a desperate lot. And that Ma Manky, whoever she is. I mean, look at her! Is that a criminal face or what? That's it! That's the answer! I get out of here, track her down, make a citizen's arrest, and bring her and her gang of thugs to justice and claim the reward. See? Easy.'

'URURURURUR . . .'

'Shut *up*, Burk,' snapped Ratsy. He turned to Nev and patted him gently on the shoulder. 'That's an ambitious plan you got there, Nev. 'Course, if you could carry it off, you'd be Mr Popularity. A lot of folks'd thank the Teller who put Big Ma Manky be'ind bars. There's plenty have had a try. Fortune hunters and such. They do say she eats 'em. Oh yes. Don't be fooled by that there picture. Big Ma's a legend in these parts. Tough as they come.'

'Oh,' said Nev. Suddenly, he felt a bit doubtful. 'I don't suppose you'd be interested in joining forces? Maybe the three of us could . . . ?'

'Well, you know, that just might be possible,' nodded Ratsy. 'But of course, there ain't no point in discussin' it until we gets out of 'ere. First things first, eh?'

'Sssh!' said Nev, suddenly holding up one finger. 'Listen.'

There came a scrabbling, snuffling noise from the small, barred window high above. All three looked up, startled. A tangle of hair appeared, framing a wet, black nose.

'Spot!' shouted Nev, leaping to his feet. 'It's Spot! He's tracked me down! Hey, Spot! Are you all right, boy?'

'That's your dog, I take it?' enquired Ratsy.

'It most certainly is! He's jolly intelligent, too. Come to think of it, there just might be a way he can get us out of here.'

'Yeah? What, like, get up a petition?'

'No, no! I'm serious. Look, he's still got the rope around his neck. We can slip it off him and *tie one end to the bars, see?*'

' 'E's gone, Nev,' said Ratsy. But Nev was so carried away with his idea that he didn't hear.

'Then I send him off to get Venetia. Then I can make a—a sort of lassoo and *throw it over Venetia's saddle!*'

' 'E's gone, Nev.'

'. . . and then she could pull *the bars out and . . .* what?'

'The mutt. 'E's gone.'

'Of course he hasn't *gone.* Spot? Where are you, boy?'

But Ratsy was right. The small, barred window was empty.

'Oh,' said Nev, brokenly. 'That's that, then.'

'Never mind, kid,' said Ratsy. 'It was a lousy idea anyway. The window's too small to get out. It'd 'ave to be bigger, see? An' there's only one way to make that window bigger.'

'What's that?' asked Nev.

A mighty blast resounded. Nev's teeth rattled in his skull. A split second later, he was lifted off his feet and hurled backwards against the far wall.

Bricks whizzed past his nose and falling bars clanged around him. Sooty plaster dust rained down into his hair. Choking and spluttering, he attempted to clear his eyes.

'Dynamite,' said Ratsy, in the sudden silence that followed.

'URURURURURURUR!' bellowed Burk—but this time, it had a celebratory sound.

Dazed with shock, Nev peered upwards at what had once been the small, barred window. The window was no more. Instead, there was a large, jagged hole through which the night wind blew—and standing there, grinning down at them through a mouthful of blackened teeth, with Spot clamped firmly beneath one arm and the other hand holding a club with nails in, was the tiniest little old lady Nev had ever seen.

'Wotcher, boys,' said Big Ma Manky, cheerfully. 'Ready to ride?'

Whooping with glee, Ratsy swung himself up through the hole, closely followed by Burk. There was a bit of back slapping, then the three of them stood staring down at Nev, who stared right back through a faceful of soot.

'Who's this?' demanded Ma Manky.

'That's young Nev, Ma,' explained Ratsy. 'Banged up through no fault of 'is own. Needs to get 'ome to 'is gran in a hurry. Bit of a domestic crisis.' He bent down and mumbled in Ma's ear.

'Well, well,' said Ma Manky. 'Is that so? Well now, son, seems to me ya

111

could do with a spot of help. Ain't right, a fine young lad like yaself parted from his dear old granny. How 'bout an escort home?'

With a grin, she reached down and extended a hand.

Nev hesitated for just one split second—then reached up and gripped it.

The warden came running when he heard the explosion—but he was too late, of course. All he found was an empty cell with a gaping hole opening into the street. And—rather to his surprise—the sack of fake coins. Oh, and a scorched, very grubby postcard. It was addressed to Plumtree Cottage, Fingle Forest. This is what it said:

So, reader. Does he make it? Find out in the next *gripping instalment . . .*

115